SO-ARN-269

GRANDMOTHER STORIES

OF

THE NORTHWEST

by Nashone

Illustrations by Ross Coates

Sierra Oaks Publishing Company
1987

Copyright © 1987

Sierra Oaks Publishing Company
1370 Sierra Oaks Court
Newcastle, California   95658-9791

All rights reserved
Printed in the United States of America

ISBN: 0-940113-06-6

To my mother and father, with love

Table of Contents

INTRODUCTION

In the Pacific Northwest, Indians and white people did not always get along with one another. But sometimes they did, and sometimes they became good friends. That was the case for a white man named Lucullus V. McWhorter. He was a rancher in the Yakima Valley, and he became a close friend to many Northwestern Indians.

The Indians called McWhorter *Hemene Kawan* or "Old Wolf." They respected him and shared their victories and sorrows with him. They also shared their oral traditions, stories, and legends with the friendly cowboy. During the first half of this century, the Indians told McWhorter hundreds of stories. To the Indians these are sacred legends and truths, not "myths" as some white people have labelled them.

Through the stories the Indians relate their history and their close bond with plants and animals, rivers and mountains, winds and thunder. Their past was handed down through stories, like the ones presented here. These Grandmother stories are authentic, told to McWhorter by tribal elders and preserved in Holland Library, Washington State University.

The first story, "The Dead Canoeman of the Columbia: Origin of the Sitting Rock," is a Wasco Indian story. It was recorded in July, 1912 and offered to McWhorter in much the

same manner presented here. Unfortunately,
the rancher does not tell us who gave him this
story.   The second chapter is taken from a
story shared by the Klickitat, Cascade,
Wishram, and Wasco Indians.   McWhorter
recorded the legend on July 4, 1918 and
entitled the manuscript "Battle of the *Attiyiyi*
and *Toqueenut.*"

The third story is likely a Yakima legend,
but McWhorter failed to report who gave him
the oral tradition or when he recorded an
essay he called "*Aloquat* and *Tweetash* Contend
Over the Division of Light and Darkness." The
fourth chapter is Yakima and Wasco in origin.
An Indian named Blazing Bush told McWhorter
the story while the two men rode horseback in
the woods along the upper reaches of Ahtanum
Creek on the Yakima Reservation.

The final story, "Bridge of the Gods," is a
Wasco story narrated by *Anawhoa* (Black Bear)
to McWhorter in September, 1914.   The
author presents five stories, since five is the
sacred number of many Northwestern Indians.
Although the stories have been presented in a
fictionalized form, they are true to the
originals in most respects.   These Indian
stories are set in the Inland Northwest in the
present-day states of Washington and Oregon.

The Indians of the Great Columbia
Plateau lived near the Columbia, Yakima,
Snake, and other rivers. They believed in the
sacredness of the mother earth and the fish,
game, roots, and berries. They believe in a
Creator and the importance of the Creator's
laws.   The beliefs of the Indians and their
relationship with the land is evident in these
stories. The legends presented in this book

are offered in the hope that the young and young at heart will come to understand the history, culture, religion, literature, and society of the Plateau Indians of the Northwest.

...a small group of children gathered around
Grandmother...

CHAPTER ONE

The cold wind blew across the mountains, sweeping down onto the Plateau from the north and west, where the ice lived most of the year around. The children playing in the field quickly turned their backs to the wind, squeezing their eyes tightly shut as their hair blew around their faces. It was still autumn on the calendar, but winter was making itself felt early in the Northwest. The parents and grandparents of these children had already taken precautions against a fierce winter, fastening storm windows into place and laying in firewood. The children were all bundled in heavy coats and warm gloves, with knitted hats on their heads.

As the strong force of the wind began to die away, one of the boys yelled at the others, "C'mon, start the game!"

The rest of the boys and girls turned back to the game they were playing with the large, round ball that was kicked between two groups of the children. But before the game began, one of the boys stopped to stare down the narrow road which lined the field. Thomas Jim thought he saw the frail figure of his elderly aunt making her way up the hill. She was the grandmother of his cousins, Annie and Charlie, but Thomas loved her and thought of her as though she were his own grandmother. These days she seemed to be sick more often than she used to be, and it was a special occasion when she appeared at his house or the house of his cousins.

Thomas loved to stay close to Grandmother whenever she came around. Grandmother was full of stories about the Animal People and the old days, before the white man came, before even the Indian People had been placed on the earth. She would tell the children these stories over and over again, until they thought they had learned the story by heart. Then one of them would try to repeat the tale exactly the way Grandmother had told it. Grandmother would listen to the child very carefully, and when the story was finished she would gently correct any errors the child had made. The child would then tell the story again, usually without repeating the mistakes.

Thomas remembered the first story he had recited to Grandmother. He had been very small and the story was a short one, but Grandmother had encouraged him to try to tell it to the small group of children that had gathered around her. It was the story of the dead canoeman of the Columbia River.

"It was in the early time," Thomas had said in a quiet voice. "It was in the days of the Animal People, near what is today the town of Lyle, Washington. A man and his wife once canoed down the *Chiawana*, which means 'Big Water.' We call it the Columbia River today."

Thomas had paused for a moment, thinking about the beginning of the story and remembering the words Grandmother had used. When he began again, the story came very naturally to him. This is the way he told the story.

...it looked to the wife as if her husband was dead...

While they were on the water, the man became very sleepy and wanted to rest. So he told his wife, "Let me sleep on your lap. Do not be afraid, and no matter what you see, do not believe that I am dead." His wife agreed and the man put his head on his wife's lap.

The man was very tired and he quickly went into a deep sleep. After awhile it looked to the wife as if her husband was dead. Worms began to creep out of his shoulders, falling onto the woman's lap. The woman became sure that her husband was dead. The husband had told her not to believe he was dead, but the woman pushed his head off of her lap anyway. The man suddenly awoke.

"Why did you not believe me?" the man cried. "Why did you throw me out of your lap?"

"Because you are dead," the wife replied, "and I was afraid."

Then the man put his wife on an eagle feather and threw her into a cave in a smooth cliff along the Columbia River. The woman turned to stone and is still there today.

When Thomas had finished his story there was silence for a moment, then Grandmother had smiled at him. She had praised him for his memory, and he smiled proudly when she told him that she would make no corrections in his story.

Thomas now knew for certain that it was Grandmother making her way carefully down the sidewalk. He left the game with a holler to his friends that his grandmother was coming to visit. A few of the children who also liked listening to Grandmother's stories broke away from the game, too, and followed Thomas as he ran toward the old woman.

"Grandmother!" he cried as he drew near her. "Will you be staying at my house tonight?"

The woman stopped and waited for the boy to reach her before answering. She used a cane to help her walk these days, but her face was as peaceful as ever. She wore a smile to welcome the children.

"Yes, Thomas. Your parents have invited me to have dinner with you."

Thomas did not try to hide his excitement. "Will you tell us some stories, Grandmother? It has been a long time since you have told us your stories."

"And it has been a long time since you told me one of my stories back," she replied. "Tonight will be a good night for the telling of stories."

*The Salmon chief kept slipping…unable to stand
securely on his feet…*

CHAPTER TWO

After the family had finished eating dinner that night, while the grown-ups were cleaning up the dishes and putting away the leftover food, Grandmother sat beside the wood-burning stove, surrounded by children. The cold wind continued to whistle its way through the cracks in the walls and doorways. Occasionally a leafless branch of a tree would scrape against a window. The fire warmed the room with its crackling flames. About half a dozen children huddled at Grandmother's feet, some laying on pillows, others wrapped in blankets for extra warmth. Grandmother sat with her eyes lightly closed, her normal pose before she began telling a story. The children waited expectantly.

Grandmother began her story without ceremony. She reminded the children that when the Creator first put living beings on the earth, the Animal People were equal. They could talk to each other like members of different tribes. Grandmother said that in the old days animals had more human qualities than they do today. The Indians of the present time came later, but they had learned the stories of the first Animal People and passed them down from parent to child.

During that time of the Animal People, there were five brothers who were the Wolves, or the *Lalawish*. They saw that *Toqeenut*, the Chief of the Salmon People and of all other fish, was a strong and powerful ruler, and they were very jealous of him. So the Wolves began to spread lies about Salmon Chief, saying bad things about him. Salmon Chief's followers, the Salmon People, then began to spread bad stories about the Wolves. Hard feelings grew between the Wolf People and the Salmon People, and five Wolf brothers prepared to fight the Salmon.

A great Chief of the Coyote People at that time was named *Speelyi*, and he was saddened by the approaching war. He said to himself, "I cannot stop the Animal People from fighting, for I am helpless to prevent a war. So rather than stand by and just watch, I will fight, too. I will fight for the Wolves."

The news spread quickly that the Wolf brothers were going to fight the Salmon Chief and the Chinook Salmon People. When the news reached the cold, far north, the *Attiyiyi* listened with great interest. The five brothers who were known as the *Attiyiyi* were the icy, cold wind which blows from the northeast. No one could stand before this wind, because it is the most deadly of all winds. These brothers were the enemies of Salmon Chief, because the Salmon People loved the warm, southwesterly wind which came at the end of winter. The warm wind melted the snow and ice, and it was then that the Salmon swam up the river.

The North Wind brothers said, "We will be there to fight for the Wolves."

The five North Wind brothers and the five Wolf brothers met to discuss how they would defeat the Salmon People. The North Wind brothers had already decided on a plan.

"We will wrestle with Salmon Chief," they

told the Wolves. "We can wrestle with him and throw him down. Then there will be ice and cold over the *Chiawana*, cold will be everywhere." Grandmother reminded the children that the *Chiawana* is known today as the Columbia River.

The Wolves liked the plan of the North Wind brothers. They said, "When you throw Salmon Chief down, we will fight and kill all of his children. We will make sure that none of them will survive."

So word went out to the Salmon People, calling them to gather on the ice of the Columbia River. Salmon Chief told his people, "I cannot help this, my people," he said sadly. "I cannot refuse this fight, so we will all go together to meet these boasting brothers."

At the river, the Salmon People took their places on one side of the river and their enemies lined up on the other side. Each group was prepared for the fight. Finally, the Wolf brothers spoke.

"This is a trial of strength. Salmon Chief, you must wrestle with each of the brothers of the cold North Wind, beginning with the oldest and going down to the youngest."

Salmon Chief was afraid of these brothers from the North, but he knew that he must fight or he would lose face with his people. He turned to his wife and children, trying to smile. But his heart was heavy with sadness, because he believed that his life would soon be ending, and that his family and his people were in danger.

"I am afraid," he told his family. "I do not trust the North Wind or the Wolves. Be careful! If you see I am about to be beaten, you must run away quickly and hide!"

The Wolves called out for the match to begin. Salmon Chief and the oldest brother of the North Wind were stripped and ready for wrestling as they walked out onto the ice-covered river. The brothers of the North Wind were able to stand on the ice, but Salmon Chief kept slipping and sliding, unable to stand securely on his feet. Still, Salmon Chief was able to throw the oldest brother down, because he was not very strong. When Salmon Chief beat the North Wind brother, a victory cry came from the Salmon side of the river: "Ow-ow-ow-ow-ow-o-oo!" But the supporters of the Wolves and of the cold North Wind remained silent.

The second North Wind brother was a little stronger than the first, but Salmon Chief was still able to throw him down onto the ice. Again, the Salmon People gave the long shout of triumph, and the North Wind and Wolves remained quiet.

Despite these victories, Salmon Chief had doubts about his ability to win the wrestling match. "I will die," he thought, "I know I will die! There are five against one, and that is too many for me. The North Wind is too strong for me and I will die!"

The third brother of the North Wind stepped forth, stronger than his two older brothers. He quickly threw Salmon Chief hard onto the ice, dragging the Chief on the ice and killing him on the shore of the frozen Columbia River. The enemy camp yelled: "Ow-ow-ow-ow-ow-o-oo!"

Suddenly the five Wolf brothers attacked the Salmon People, killing all of the young children. The Coyotes and the Foxes joined the Wolves, first killing Salmon Chief's wife. Splitting open her belly, they found a large supply of eggs which spilled out and scattered onto a flat rock. The rest of the Salmon were killed without a struggle.

On the other side of the river, the cry of "Ow-ow-ow-ow-ow-o-oo!" rang out. The five North Wind brothers began to shout, "The Salmon People are no more! Now we will have cold all of the time! There will be ice on the Columbia River forever more!"

Coyote Chief began to realize that he had made a mistake. "I was wrong to help the Wolves," he thought. "They have killed a good man and destroyed a good people. Now the warm wind will not blow, and we will be cold from now on."

The Wolves were not finished, however. They called their followers over to the flat rock and ordered them to destroy the salmon eggs which had spilled out of Salmon Chief's wife.

Coyote Chief tried to urge the Animal People to stop their destruction. "We have killed a good man, a good Chief," he cried. "I am ashamed of what we have done." But no one listened to him.

The followers of the five Wolf brothers began to sing, "We have killed all of the Salmon! We have done a great thing! Now it will be cold all of the time!"

All of the Salmon eggs were smashed and destroyed except for one which fell into a deep crack in the flat rock. Try as they might, the Wolves and their followers could not reach the egg. The Wolf brothers were very worried about this egg, because they feared it would

one day come to life and a new line of Salmon
People would rise up. The Wolves tried so
hard to reach the egg that they made two deep
tracks in the rock. Grandmother told the
children that these tracks can be seen to this
day, in the rock near the Tumwater at Wishom.

Finally the Wolves gave up, reasoning that
since the egg was dry, it must be dead and
unable to grow. The five brothers left for the
mountains. The five North Wind brothers
stayed for awhile on the Columbia, in an icy
rock cave at Wahpeus, where they celebrated
their victory. They were happy that it would
be cold all of the time. The next day, these
brothers returned to their home in the north.

Clouds began to materialize quickly,
becoming darker and darker. The rain began
to fall and the Creator helped the one Salmon
egg which lay in the crack in the flat rock.
The egg began to swell, and as the rain fell for
five days and five nights, the water filled the
crack and lifted the egg out of the rock. The
Creator breathed life into the little egg, and at
the end of the five days a fish emerged from
the egg. On the sixth day it entered the river,
travelling to the mouth of the river near the
ocean. The little Salmon grew as it swam
along. At the mouth of the river the small fish
found his grandmother, the mother of Salmon
Chief.

The Salmon Chief's mother had heard of
her son's murder at the hands of the North
Wind, and she recognized her grandson
immediately.

"My grandson." she said, "your father was
killed by the North Wind brothers, as was his
wife, and his children, and all of his followers.

...try as they did, the Wolves and their followers
could not reach the egg...

You are the only one who has survived, and I am glad that you have come to me."

Holding her grandson close to her, Salmon Chief's mother told the little fish about his people. Finally, the boy-fish spoke.

"Tell me how my father and mother were killed. Tell me how I was saved, and how I am alive today."

So Salmon Chief's mother told her grandson all that she knew, ending her story with these words: "Grandson, I will help you grow fast and strong, so that one day you can stand against these brothers in the spring and beat them in a wrestling match as they beat your father!"

Every morning the old woman made the little Salmon boy bathe in the cold winter water, so that he would become strong. He also worked hard at his exercises. For six moons, he practiced lifting heavy objects to strengthen his legs. He practiced running and throwing and jumping, so that his body grew larger and his muscles became firm and truly powerful. The old woman watched him grow with satisfaction.

"I am happy," she told him often. "You will be stronger than my son, your father. You will not fall before the cold North Wind."

At the same time, the young Salmon's mind grew strong, too. Each day, as he exercised, he told himself over and over that the North Wind would not defeat him, that he would destroy the five North Wind brothers as they had murdered his father and his people.

Spring arrived, when the Salmon were supposed to run, but the snow and ice remained on the ground. The North Wind brothers would not allow the warmth of the southern wind to bring an end to the winter cold. The young Salmon left his tipi and called out to his grandmother's mat lodge.

"Come look at me now, Grandmother!" he shouted.

When Salmon Chief's mother emerged from her home, she was pleased to see how big and strong her grandson had become. As she watched, he walked over to a small thicket of trees and pulled them out of the ground easily.

"That's right," the old woman cried. "That is how you can tell you are really strong. But you must wait two moons more. Then you will be strong enough to defeat the North Wind."

So the young Salmon continued to bathe in the cold river water and to exercise every day. Soon he was able to twist trees out of the ground that were the size of his arms. His grandmother watched with pride, thinking that her son was never as strong as this boy. At the end of two months, he was able to pull up trees that fifty men could not shake! One day he picked up a large rock which sat near his grandmother's mat lodge and threw it into the middle of the Columbia. The ice on the surface of the water cracked and the rock sank to the bottom of the river.

"You are ready now," said the old woman with a smile. "You can beat the five North Wind brothers. Five baskets of oil to pour on the ice will give you secure footing on the smoothest of ice, and you will be able to stand firm and tall against each one of those brothers."

"Thank you, Grandmother," the boy said.

...as she watched, Young Chinook pulled the trees out of the ground...

"Because you are going to fight these brothers, the cold wind from the north, you will have a new name. I will call you *Wenowyyi,* which means 'Young Chinook Wind.' You are the warm wind coming from the ocean, to drive away the cold." Tears filled the old woman's eyes as she watched her grandson with pride.

"Don't worry, Grandmother," Young Chinook said gently as he held her in a close embrace. "I will fix these boastful North Wind brothers! Prepare the five baskets of oil and I will be on my way."

Now the North Wind brothers had a slave woman who was the younger sister of Salmon Chief's mother, and they treated her very badly. The crippled sister of the North Wind was especially cruel to the slave woman. Young Chinook learned from his grandmother that her sister was nearly starved, because her masters gave her little food, and nearly frozen, because her clothes were only thin rags. She had almost died twice because of the cruel treatment.

"My sister will tell you all about the oil," the old woman said to Young Chinook. "She will fix it for you. Now go, my grandson. I know you will beat the North Wind on the ice."

Young Chinook walked to the place where he would fight the brothers. As he approached the Cascades, he began to grab huge trees and pull them out of the ground. He tossed large boulders into the river like pebbles. With each step Young Chinook concentrated on the upcoming battle, struggling to maintain the physical strength he had worked so hard to gain. But in addition,

Young Chinook knew he had to keep a strong mind and a positive attitude. Over and over he repeated the same thoughts.

"Nothing can defeat me!" he thought. "I am Young Chinook! I am stronger than my father was, and the cold wind cannot survive before my breath! I will throw them on the ice of the Columbia River and I will kill this cold. It will not stay cold forever."

Young Chinook continued to travel along the Columbia and approached Celilo Falls, where the North Wind brothers lived in a rock cave. As he drew nearer, the warmth of the Chinook wind preceded him. The warm wind passed into the mat lodge where the Salmon boy's old aunt sat, cold and starving, and melted the icicles which hung from her hair. She was waiting at the door when Young Chinook arrived at her lodge.

"I knew it was you!" she cried. "I knew the son of Salmon Chief would return one day to drive away the cold!"

Young Chinook embraced his aunt, feeling how weak and cold she was, and he was more determined than ever to destroy these cruel brothers. The old aunt told Young Chinook how the crippled sister of the North Wind beat her every day, and she showed him bruises on her arms and back.

"Don't worry," Young Chinook told the old lady, "after tomorrow she will not bother you again." The two ate a small meal and then went to sleep.

Early in the morning, Young Chinook took a thorny rose bush and hid near the door of his aunt's lodge. The crippled sister could not see him as she entered the old woman's lodge, and as she limped toward the old woman, Young Chinook silently crept behind her. Just when the crippled woman raised her arm to strike the aunt, Young Chinook took the thorny bush and struck the crippled sister of the North Wind hard on the back. She limped as fast as she could out of the lodge, screaming loudly and leaving a trail of blood behind her. She hurried to her brothers and told them what had happened.

"Yes," the oldest of the brothers said, nodding his head, "last night the warm wind came near and we were afraid."

"It is the Salmon Chief come to life again!" cried another brother. "He has come to meet us on the ice of the Columbia!"

So the North Wind brothers sent word to all of the Animal People, urging everyone to come see the great wrestling match. The five Wolf Brothers came from the mountains, and all the big chiefs came, like the chiefs of the Foxes and Birds, bringing their people with them. Everyone was very excited and looked forward to the spectacular wrestling match.

Young Chinook arrived with his five baskets of oil, and the old aunt followed closely so that she could help him during the match. The North Wind brothers watched him approach and they were confident that they would beat him as they had beaten his father.

"We are strong," they whispered to each other, "and there are five of us against one of him. It will be easy to kill this boasting Salmon boy."

The North Wind brothers were so sure of themselves that they called out to Young Chinook in a friendly voice. "Hello!" they cried.

"Have you come to wrestle with us, friend?"

"I have," Young Chinook called back in return. "I will beat you on the ice of the Columbia!"

By mid-day, crowds of people lined the banks of the frozen river to watch the match. The crippled sister was also in the crowd. Coyote Chief stood among the crowd, pleased that Young Chinook had come to challenge the cold North Wind. He was tired of the cold, and proud that one of Salmon Chief's children had survived. Coyote Chief saw immediately that Young Chinook had become even stronger than Salmon Chief had been.

Finally, the North Wind brothers and Young Chinook stepped out onto the ice. Young Chinook Wind turned to the old aunt and said, "Follow me out onto the ice."

His aunt nodded. "When you reach the place where you will fight, I will pour a basket of oil on the ice. Then you can stand strong on the ice, without slipping."

The North Wind brothers watched the old aunt, who had been their slave woman, pour the oil on the ice and they laughed loudly. "What is this?" the youngest brother shouted. "Will this old slave perform magic with her oil?" Part of the crowd laughed with the brothers, but many remained silent, because they wanted Young Chinook to win. They were tired of the cold weather.

Young Chinook looked strong as he waited for the oldest brother to step out on the ice, a result of the months of exercise and training. The five Wolf brothers looked at each other nervously, afraid that their protectors might lose to this young Salmon boy.

The oldest North Wind brother was hardly on the ice before Young Chinook was able to throw him down hard and knock him unconscious. The Wolf brothers dragged him off the ice as Coyote Chief let out a long cry of victory.

"Ow-ow-ow-ow-ow-o-oo!" he howled. It was very quiet on the enemy side of the river.

The second brother stepped forward, remembering his match with Salmon Chief. He watched suspiciously as the old aunt poured oil at Young Chinook's feet. Although this brother was a little stronger, Young Chinook was able to throw him down without much trouble. Once again Coyote Chief howled the cry of victory, making the Wolves grumble because the great Chief was now against them.

The third brother came forward to match his skill and strength with that of the mighty Young Chinook, as the old aunt poured the third basket of oil at his feet. This time the Salmon boy faced more of a fight, but finally he was able to lift the brother over his head. Three times Young Chinook turned him over his head, then slammed him down on the ice. The brother was knocked unconscious and had to be dragged off the ice by the Wolves.

"Ow-ow-ow-ow-ow-o-oo!" howled Coyote Chief.

Now the two youngest brothers were frightened. They had not fought Salmon Chief in the first match, and Young Chinook was stronger than his father. Coyote Chief's people began to call out to the remaining brothers.

"Hurry up!" they shouted. "Hurry up and fight! We cannot stand here waiting for you all

...Young Chinook lifted the third North Wind
brother over his head...

day!"

The fourth brother came out slowly onto the ice, as the fourth basket of oil was poured at the Salmon boy's feet. Young Chinook looked him squarely in the eye and noticed that the North Wind brother was shaking. But he was stronger than the other brothers, and Young Chinook had to concentrate hard to beat him. But in the end, this brother also lay unconscious on the ice.

"Ow-ow-ow-ow-ow-o-oo!" came the cry of victory. Most of the Animal People were now cheering wildly for Young Chinook.

Young Chinook was tired. Although he had beaten the first four North Wind brothers, it had taken every ounce of his strength to keep fighting. Now he faced the youngest and strongest of the brothers, and although this brother was scared, he had a determined look in his eye. Young Chinook knew that this brother would fight with all of his might. In the crowd, the tension mounted.

This match was very close, and several times the crowd thought that the North Wind might win after all. But finally Young Chinook lifted the North Wind brother above his head and threw him hard onto the ice. The Wolves dragged him off as the crowd cheered.

"Ow-ow-ow-ow-ow-o-oo!" they cried. "Young Chinook, son of Salmon Chief, the Chief of the Chinooks, has won!"

But in the midst of the confusion, the lame sister of the North Wind brothers ran crying into the Columbia River, escaping through a hole in the ice. As Coyote Chief stepped onto a high rock and the people drew close to hear his words, the Wolves fled into the Cascade Mountains. They knew that they had been defeated and that their day of glory had ended.

Coyote Chief looked out at the Animal People that thronged around him. He stood thoughtfully for a moment as he decided what he would say.

"We have beaten the bad people," he said, "and now it will be warm again. We will have nice rich food, and the salmon will run again. But the crippled sister of the North Wind has escaped, and for that reason we must have a little cold for a short time each year. But not cold as it has been."

At that moment the warm wind of the Chinook started to blow and the ice began to melt.   As the crowd began to disperse, Coyote Chief turned to Young Chinook and in a low voice said, "Young Chinook, I have something to tell you. One day there will be a different kind of people living here, from here to Wahpeus to Skein. People will live from the mouth of the Columbia to the ocean. They will not be Animal People or Bird People. And there will be plenty for everyone to eat. And when these people gather and play games, the winners will cry out: Ow-ow-ow-ow-ow-o-oo! And the losers will remain silent."

As Grandmother finished her story of the Battle between the five North Wind brothers and the Salmon People, the children were still listening to her every word. It had been a long story, longer than most, but also an exciting one.

Thomas was the first to speak. "Is that why the warm wind comes and melts the snow each spring?"

Grandmother nodded in reply. "Do you know what the victory cry of Coyote Chief is?" she asked. Before any of the children could answer, she raised her hand to her mouth and as she let out a high yell, she quickly beat the palm of her hand against her mouth. "That is the cry of a winner," she said in a warning tone of voice, "and should never be used by a loser. But this is enough for one night. Perhaps tomorrow we will have another story."

The sleepy children smiled at the thought of it.

...*Grizzly Bear became very upset at the message of Frog brothers*...

CHAPTER THREE

Thomas picked up another piece of wood from the long stack of chopped firewood which leaned against the house, placing it on top of the tall pile of wood already in his arms. His house, like those of most of his friends and relatives, could not provide enough protection against the cold wind. The white man's electricity was too expensive to use by itself to keep the drafty house warm during the winter. It was only natural for Thomas and his family to use wood, a gift of their mother earth and an old source of fuel. It was also more affordable.

Stepping carefully to avoid spilling his bundle of chopped firewood, Thomas filled the empty box which sat next to the large wood-burning stove. His morning chores completed, Thomas moved to the kitchen where Grandmother was helping his mother prepare breakfast. It had been late when Grandmother finished telling her story the night before, and the cold wind had been blowing so strongly that Thomas' parents had urged Grandmother to spend the night at their home. Thomas had been delighted, hoping for a chance to hear yet another story. But now the boy was hungry and he focused his attention on the eggs, bacon, and pancakes covered with huckleberry preserves which waited on the table.

Thomas swallowed the last bite of huckleberries and pancakes that his stomach could take. It was Saturday, a pleasant contrast to the weekday breakfasts that were gobbled up as the family hurried off to school and to work. Coffee cups were refilled and the family lingered in the warm, comfortable kitchen. Thomas waited until there was a lull in the conversation, then quickly moved to capture his grandmother's attention.

"Grandmother, will you please tell us another story?" he asked.

She smiled at the eager boy. "Which one would you like to hear, Thomas?" she asked.

He frowned thoughtfully as he considered several stories. Thomas knew that he could repeat these stories well, but they were not letter perfect. He was still too uncertain to recite them to Grandmother, so he wanted her to tell one. Finally he gave her his answer.

"The story about the division of light and darkness," he finally said.

"Alright," said Grandmother, and she launched into the story without hesitation.

Before People lived on the earth, five Frog brothers travelled down the Yakima River from the big lake that used to be called *Kecheless*. They were accompanied by the Grizzly Bear. After awhile the group reached what is now called Union Gap, and the five Frogs climbed to the top of a rocky point on the west side of the Gap. Grizzly Bear thought for a moment, then climbed to the top of the mountain on the east side of Union Gap.

As Grizzly Bear sat on top of the mountain, he thought about how tired he was from his journey, and how nice it would be to take a long rest. He gave a deep sigh, then settled down into a comfortable position.

Suddenly, the voices of the five Frogs drifted across the Gap, interrupting Grizzly Bear's peaceful thoughts.

"One night! One night! One night!" cried the Frogs. Clearly they were warning Grizzly Bear that his rest period would last only for the length of one night.

Grizzly Bear became very upset at the message of the Frog brothers, because he liked to sleep for a long time when he finally settled down to rest. "One night will not do!" he thought in agitation. "There must be a longer time for us to sleep."

"One night! One night!" repeated the song of the Frogs.

"Ten years night, come daylight! Ten years night, come daylight," Grizzly Bear sang in reply. His deep voice thundered across the Gap, but despite the strength of his voice, the Frogs were too quick for him. They could speak much faster than Grizzly Bear. Since the Frogs outnumbered Grizzly Bear by five to one, their noise was continuous and unbroken. Try as he might, Grizzly Bear could not keep up.

"One night! One night! One night!" the Frogs continued to sing.

Grizzly Bear was persistent, too. He bellowed as fast as he could, "Ten years night, come daylight. Ten years night, come daylight."

The Frogs continued to sing tirelessly, but Grizzly Bear was worn out. Finally he could stand it no more! He jumped down the mountain, creating a flat place where he landed about half way down the bluff. From there he slid to the bottom, swam across the Yakima River, and ran up the mountain to the

Frogs' camp.

The Frogs were too clever for him, though. Hearing Grizzly Bear's loud footsteps, they hopped away before he could reach them. Hopping down the north side of the mountain, the five brothers hid in the mud of Ahtanum Creek. Grizzly Bear followed them, but by the time he reached the water, the Frogs had disappeared. He waded into the water and dug through the mud with his large hands, but to no avail. Dejected, Grizzly Bear returned to the flat place in his mountain and began to sing his song.

"Ten years night, come daylight. Ten years night, come daylight."

Immediately the Frogs chanted in reply, "One night! One night! One night!"

Grizzly Bear was angrier than ever, believing that the Frogs were taunting him. He lept down the mountain, chasing the Frogs into the mud of Ahtanum Creek. As he reached the water's edge, the five brothers dove into the water and burrowed deeply into the mud. Grizzly Bear was so angry that if he had caught the elusive Frogs, he might have killed them. He tore into the water and thrust his hairy arms into the mud, but again he could not find them. Finally, he returned to his flat place all wet and covered with mud.

And so it went, Grizzly Bear singing for ten years of night followed by ten years of daylight, and the Frogs insisting on a much shorter night. Grizzly Bear would take it for as long as possible, then he would chase the Frogs into Ahtanum Creek. But he never could catch the quicker animals. Finally, Grizzly Bear was ready to compromise.

"I am tired," he thought. "I will settle on five years of night and five years of daylight." So he began to sing, "Five years night, come daylight. Five years night, come daylight."

But the energetic Frogs sang back, "One night! One night! One night!" until Grizzly Bear could stand it no more. He raced across the Gap and up the mountain, but the Frogs had long since retreated to Ahtanum Creek. Grizzly Bear was unable to dig them out of the mud, and he returned to his flat place in the mountain, muddy and wet.

So it continued for five days and five nights: the Frogs sang for a short night, Grizzly Bear gave chase, the Frogs hid in the mud of Ahtanum Creek. Finally, Grizzly Bear was ready to admit defeat. He was exhausted, unable to speak as quickly as the five Frog brothers. If he had won, he could have slept for five or ten years, then enjoyed five or ten years of daylight. But since the Frogs won, the time for rest was limited to one night. Grizzly Bear was allowed to sleep longer only during the months of winter.

When Grandmother had finished her story, she couldn't resist the urge to tease Thomas a little bit. Looking at the boy with a smile she asked, "Did I tell this story correctly, Thomas?"

The young boy had silently recited the story along with the old woman, and was proud at how accurately he had remembered it. As he nodded in reply to Grandmother's question, he wondered if one day he would tell it to children of his own.

Unable to bear the suspense of waiting... Coyote
untied the pack... (and)... the spirits of Coyote's
loved ones flew back to the Creator...

CHAPTER FOUR

The rest of the family began leaving the table, some clearing away the dishes, others going outside to play or attend to chores. But Grandmother seemed content to stay at the table, and Thomas lingered there as well.

"Thomas," she said, "why don't you tell me a story, one that you have memorized?"

"Alright," said Thomas, his mind racing to find the story he could recite without error, or at least without too many mistakes. He decided on the story of how Coyote lost immortality to the tribe. It was not long, and he had heard the story many times.

Coyote was living around the upper waters of the Ahtanum River, near what was now the Yakima Reservation, and he was sad because so many of his people were dead. He cried day in and day out, longing to see his family and friends who had passed over to the Spirit Land. Coyote finally he decided to travel across the five mountains to ask the Creator for help.

"Many of my People are dead," said Coyote to the Creator. "My heart is sad that they are gone from me. I cry every day because I cannot see my friends who are gone. I want my people with me again, and I have come far to ask you to let them come back with me to live."

Five times Coyote asked this of the First Man. When he asked it for the fifth time,

Creator said, "Alright! I will let you take your people back with you, but you must do as I tell you. Make no mistakes!"

The Creator took a small piece of deerskin and placed a bit of the spirit of each of Coyote's dead relatives and friends in it, tying the bundle securely. He gave the pack to Coyote and said, "Take this with you to your home beyond the five mountains. Do not untie it until you reach your own country. All of your people will then be alive, to live with you forever. Do not loosen the deerskin until you have passed the five mountains."

Coyote nodded eagerly. "I will do as you tell me," he agreed. "I know the law of the five mountains and I will make no mistakes. I am lonely for my People."

Holding the bundle tightly in his hands, Coyote began his trip home. His heart was no longer heavy, for he would soon see all of his loved ones. They would stay with him always. A song of happiness sprang from his lips.

Coyote crossed the first mountain on the trail, then the second and the third mountains. After a time Coyote crossed the fourth mountain on the trail. But somewhere between the fourth and the fifth mountain something happened which dashed Coyote's hopes of a reunion with his loved ones. Coyote was so saddened by his mistake that he never spoke of it, and the People wondered long and hard how Coyote had lost immortality to the tribes.

One story says that as Coyote approached the fifth and last mountain, he heard a great noise. It seemed as though many people were talking and shouting, laughing, and singing the old songs that Coyote loved. Coyote stopped and listened. Yes! It was the voices of his friends and his family! Unable to bear the suspense of waiting until he had crossed the fifth mountain, Coyote untied the pack.

Immediately the spirits of Coyote's loved ones flew back to the Creator. Had Coyote waited until he had crossed the fifth mountain, the liberated spirits would have remained with him, returning to life and living forever. But because Coyote disobeyed the Creator, all Indians now live short·lives, and they must ultimately die.

Another version says that *Tiskai* the Skunk intercepted Coyote as he crossed the mountains. Skunk was a mean medicine man who killed all who opposed him with his stinking poison. Hoping to mislead Skunk, Coyote told him that the pack contained rare and costly items. Instead, Skunk immediately demanded that Coyote open the bundle so that he might see such magnificent things. Coyote refused until Skunk threatened to kill him. Finally, Coyote opened his bundle.

The spirits of Coyote's dead wife and children rushed out of the bundle along with the others, pausing to say good-bye. Then they vanished back over the mountains and headed toward the sunrise. Poor Coyote wailed and cried, but to no avail. He had lost immortality for the tribes.

When Thomas finished the short story, he looked at Grandmother with anticipation. He was confident that he had performed well. When Grandmother nodded her head with a small smile, he knew his story had pleased her.

A great bird lived in the West…called Nohwenah
Klah…Thunderbird!

CHAPTER FIVE

The bitter, cold winter wind eventually gave way to the warmth of the Chinook wind, melting the snow and paving the way for spring to blossom forth. Small pockets of snow still clung to the earth wherever the sun and warm wind could not touch them. But the air was filled with spring and the spirits of young and old alike lifted as tiny flowers appeared and green buds formed on the trees. The cold and dreary days had taken their toll on Grandmother, who had spent most of the winter confined to her home to preserve her meager strength. Thomas had not seen her since she had visited his family, but he was too active in school and with his friends to dwell on storytelling. It was only now, as spring returned and his parents commented on Grandmother's renewed energy, that Thomas' thoughts turned once again to Grandmother and the stories of his people.

Thomas hurried to Grandmother's house when school was over for the day. He found her sitting on the front porch in an old metal chair that creaked as Grandmother made slight rocking motions. A blanket protected her from the cold of the metal, and a shawl was pulled tightly around her shoulders. She looked old and frail, but her eyes were shining brightly as the boy came through the gate and toward her house.

"Hello, Thomas!" she called out to him.

Thomas returned the greeting with a wave and a shy smile. He was always a little embarrassed around Grandmother, afraid that his persistent interest in her stories would annoy her. The old woman's warmth never failed to reassure him that she welcomed his interest. He couldn't know that Grandmother clung to the thought that in this boy's interest in her stories lay the hope that the heritage of their people would live on for another generation.

"Hello, Grandmother," Thomas said as he sat down in a nearby chair. "Are you feeling better today?" he asked with a respectful tone.

She smiled in reply. "Well enough to tell a story with you," she said. "A story that is close to my heart. I can remember my grandfather telling it to me when I was a little girl. It was always my favorite."

Thomas settled back in anticipation, listening carefully as the story unfolded.

Grandmother began by explaining that when the earth was first created, only Animal and Bird People inhabited the land, and they were the only tribes living at that time. Some animals were great and could perform mighty wonders. One such wonder resulted in the building of the Bridge.

A great bird lived in the west, where the sun set at the end of each day, and all the People were afraid of it. It was called *Nohwenah klah* or Thunderbird. One day Thunderbird created five high mountains. Then he gathered all the people together and made an announcement.

"I have created these five mountains to keep you all away from where I live," he said.

"If anyone passes over these mountains, I will kill him. These mountains are my laws!" Then Thunderbird returned to his home in the west.

The Wolf, also known as *Halish*, was one of the greatest of animals. The five Wolf brothers did not believe Thunderbird's threat, saying, "We will go! We will be the first to see what Thunderbird will really do when we cross the mountains!"

So the Wolf brothers stood together in a row and in unison they placed their right feet over the first mountain. Nothing happened. Again in unison they stepped forward with their left feet. Thunderbird struck them dead.

When the People learned that the five Wolf brothers were dead, the five Grizzly Bear brothers, also called *Tweetiyah*, said, "We will go! We will take a chance! We will not die like the five Wolf brothers!"

So the Grizzly Bears travelled to the first of the mountains created by Thunderbird. Standing together in a row, they stepped forward with their right feet. The brothers remained unharmed. But as soon as they lifted their left feet over the mountain, the Grizzly Bear brothers fell dead. The same thing happened when the Cougar, known then as *Wyyouwee*, tried to cross the mountains, and again to the five Beaver brothers, called *Yehkah.*

Now Coyote's oldest sons were great men, greater than all the others. They told each other, "Let us go talk to the mountains, talk to this great law. We will break the law down, or see if it will break us down, so that the People may pass to where the sun sets."

The five Coyote brothers travelled to the

Coyote....found the creator waiting for him...

mountains that Thunderbird had created, and the two eldest brothers talked to the mountains. Although they were very persuasive, the mountains could only move up and down, shaking and dancing. Thunderbird had made the mountains so that they could do nothing else. The Coyote brothers were killed when they crossed over the first mountain.

The five Coyote brothers had not told their father of their plans to talk to the mountains. Coyote had instructed them never to stay away from home overnight, so when they did not return, Coyote knew in his heart that his sons were dead. Coyote was wiser than his sons, wiser than all others, because he had been taught by the Creator in the Land Above, called *Whamepommete.*. The old Coyote knew that Thunderbird was responsible for the death of his sons.

When his sons had been gone for five nights, Coyote said, "I know that my sons are all dead. Thunderbird has killed then with his five laws, the five mountains." Coyote began to cry, quietly at first and then loudly, wailing among the mountains and caverned rocks. He retreated to a lonely place, letting his grief overtake him. Coyote rolled on the ground, sad and miserable, for his heart was heavy and he was lonely. Somehow he found the strength to lift his head to the sky and pray to the Creator to save his five sons and bring them back to life. After he had been crying and praying for many hours, the answer came.

"You cannot break this great law of the Thunderbird," a Voice said to him. "You cannot go over the five mountains, the five laws. The law stands there as made by

Thunderbird."

Coyote continued to pray, as if he had not heard the Voice.   He stayed in that lonely place, rolling on the ground and crying pitifully, until the Creator was moved by the father's grief.

"There is only one way to save your sons. You must travel for five days and five nights, until you reach the Land Above. There you will be instructed on how you may be able to bring your five sons back to life."

Coyote immediately left for the Land Above. He found the Creator waiting for him.

"You are wise," said Coyote. "You know of the Thunderbird, who had made the five mountains, the five laws. No one can pass over them to reach the sunset. My five sons are dead.   I want you to give me a law, the strongest kind of law, so I can defeat Thunderbird, that the People may live in freedom."

The Creator answered Coyote, "Yes, I know of the the five mountains, the five laws of Thunderbird.   Those laws are to prevent anyone from looking on Thunderbird, who lives at the sunset."

Coyote listened to the Creator carefully, hoping for some sign that his sons might be saved.

"You are a strong man," Creator continued, "almost as strong as me. I will help you destroy the Thunderbird.   I made the earth; I made all of the animals. Some I made greater than others. Thunderbird was made the strongest. I will help you by blinding the eyes of Thunderbird. Then you can go over the five mountains, the five laws, and destroy him."

The first mountain did not completely fall… leaving
in place a great stone bridge…

"Ow-ow-ow-ow-ow-o-oo!" howled Coyote gleefully.

"Listen carefully!" Creator said. "Do you know of a great bird that lives on the earth which is called Eagle, or *Whyammah*? Eagle has powerful strength and can make law. When you return to the earth, find the youngest of Eagle's children. Pull a feather from under the wing of this youngest Eagle child, a small, downy feather. This feather has power which runs from the heart. You will find it growing near the young bird's heart."

Coyote thanked the Creator gratefully, then returned to the earth. Immediately he went to the place where Eagle lived with all of his children.

"The Creator sent me to you," Coyote said. "He gave me strength for the journey. He told me to ask you for your youngest child's feather, the light and downy feather which grows next to his heart. We need your help, for Thunderbird is killing all of the People."

Eagle immediately answered Coyote, saying, "If the Creator sent you to me, I will surely help you. I will give you my strength and my power to fight Thunderbird."

So Eagle plucked the feather from his youngest child, where it grew under the wing next to his heart. Handing it to Coyote, he explained what the old man must do to defeat the Thunderbird.

"Go ten days and ten nights without food or drink, and then you will become like this feather. Then you can travel anywhere with ease."

Coyote starved himself for ten days and ten nights and sure enough, he was turned into a feather like the one given to him by Eagle. He flew through the air towards the five mountains, but he stayed some distance away. As he moved through the air he made the sound of rolling thunder, low and rumbling, which seemed to come from the sunrise. After he repeated the sound two more times, Thunderbird heard the thunder.

"How can this be?" Thunderbird said in amazement. "Only I was given the power to make that noise, from sun to sun. This thunder must be coming from the Land Above! I must be dead! I must be dead!"

Once again Coyote made the sound of rolling thunder. Thunderbird's amazement turned to anger. "I will kill whatever makes this sound. I will kill it as it comes closer to me!"

Then Thunderbird made a mighty noise, a greater thunder which answered the sound made by Coyote. But Thunderbird could not find Coyote, who was disguised as a feather. Coyote moved higher and higher into the air, darting and whirling so rapidly that he could not be seen. Thunderbird became afraid, and he was certain that if Coyote created the fifth blast of thunder, it would mean certain death for Thunderbird.

Thunderbird dove deep into the water to escape, hearing Coyote high above him. Coyote prayed to the Creator in the Land Above for help one last time. Here was his chance to kill Thunderbird once and for all, that the people might live! His sons might come back to life! Creator heard the prayers of Coyote and had pity on him.

Thunderbird shrank deeper into the

water, scared and shaking. Coyote was still invisible, but Thunderbird knew he remained in the sky above. Coyote brought forth a fifth rumbling of thunder in a crash which sounded as though the world was bursting. The five mountains, the five laws of Thunderbird, crumbled and fell. Fragments of the mountains landed in the Columbia River, where they formed the many islands which dot the course of the river.

The first mountain did not completely fall, leaving in place a great stone bridge across the Columbia River at the Cascade Mountains. This bridge stood for hundreds of snows, no one was exactly sure for how many, and then it fell. It used to be the rule that when the ancestors of the Indians paddled their canoes past this point, no one was to look up at the rocks of this bridge. In some tribes, in fact, the Indians would land their canoes before they reached the bridge and walk around the huge natural structure, fearing that the bridge might collapse as had been prophesied by wise men. Finally the bridge did fall, confirming the prophecies.

After destroying the mountains, Coyote said to Thunderbird, "There is a new race of People coming, the Indians, and they will arrive in large numbers. You will not kill them as you have killed the present People. Once in a while you may produce a great noise, causing the earth to tremble and the People to be afraid. You can strike the trees and the high places, but you can never be as great as you were."

Then the five sons of Coyote and all of the Animal People destroyed by Thunderbird,

As long as there are young people like you Thomas…
the wisdom of the People will live on…

returned to life.

Grandmother turned to Thomas after the story was concluded and looked at him closely. "When I was a little girl," she said, "my father told me this story, and he heard it from his father, who heard it from his father and so on. I don't know when the bridge fell, but some of our ancestors did see it. I was not supposed to tell this story, not even to my own children. But I have told it to you and it is true." There were tears in Grandmother's eyes.

Thomas was still entranced by the story, honored that Grandmother had shared it with him. Hesitantly he asked, "Grandmother, why aren't these stories written down, so that our people will not forget them?"

A sad look crossed Grandmother's face. "My mother, when she became very old, used to say that the young Indians could not be depended on to tell the stories of the People in the true way, because they do not listen to the stories. She used to say that the wisdom of the People would soon be forgotten." She shrugged. "Perhaps we should write the stories down."

A breeze had begun to blow, and Grandmother pulled the shawl closer around her shoulders. Thomas looked at his feet, to avoid the disrespect of looking directly at Grandmother at such a thoughtful moment. When his Grandmother spoke again, however, Thomas could not help but meet her eyes because of the warmth in her voice.

"But as long as there are young people like you, Thomas," she said with a smile, "I know the wisdom of the People will live on."

GLOSSARY

Ahtanum Creek: Water source on the Yakima Resrvation running out of the Cascade Mountains to the east.

Attiyiyi: North Wind.

Cascade Mountains: Mountain range running down the Pacific Northwest from Canada to California.

Chiawana: Columbia River.

Chinook: The Indian name for salmon and the generally accepted name of the warm western wind in the Pacific Northwest.

Five: Sacred number of Northwestern Indians.

Hemene Kawan: Old Wolf.

Lalawish: Wolf.

McWhorter, Lucullus V.: Rancher-historian who recorded oral histories of Indians of the Pacific Northwest.

Nashone: Beautiful.

Nohwenah Klah: Thunderbird.

Plateau: Geographical region, interior of the Pacific Northwest.

Qeenut: Salmon.

Speelyi: Coyote.

Toqeenut: Chief of the Salmon.

Tweetiyah: Grizzly Bear.

Whamepommete: World Above; home of the Creator.

Whyammah: Eagle.

Yakima Reservation: Established in 1855 in central Washington and made up of many different tribes and bands.

Yakima River: Major water source for Yakima Indians; flows into the Columbia River.

The author and publisher wish to thank Andrew George, Mary Jim, and Patricia Jones for providing us an understanding of Plateau Indian culture. We also thank the educators who run the Title V, Indian Education Program in the Pacific Northwest for the excellent work they are doing on behalf of Indian people.